The Ghost Train

First published in 2011
by Wayland
This edition published in 2014

Wayland
338 Euston Road
London NW1 3BH

Wayland Australia
Level 17/207 Kent Street
Sydney, NSW 2000

Series Editor: Louise John
Editor: Katie Powell
Cover design: Paul Cherrill
Design: D.R.ink
Consultant: Shirley Bickler

A CIP catalogue record for this book is available from the British Library.

ISBN 9780750263467

Printed in China

Wayland is a division of Hachette Children's Books,
an Hachette UK Company

www.hachette.co.uk

2 4 6 8 10 9 7 5 3

The Ghost Train

Written by Liss Norton
Illustrated by Michael Garton

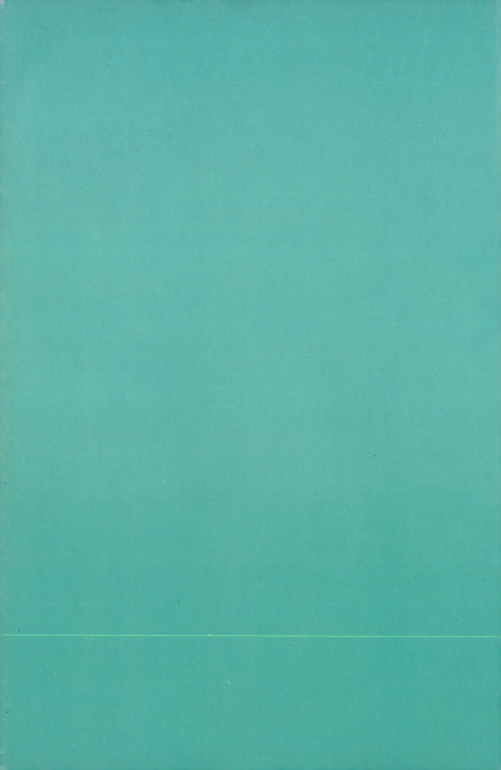

Skelly Nelly woke up one morning and looked out of her window. A fair had arrived next to Creepy Castle

"A fair!" Skelly Nelly cried. "I love fairs."

Bony Tony didn't feel the same way at all.

“I don’t want all of these people so close to Creepy Castle,” he said. “Let’s scare everyone away.”

“Oh, no! I’d like to look around first,” replied Skelly Nelly.

The fair was filled with people having lots of fun.

Skelly Nelly saw people screaming as the rollercoaster zipped up and down.

Bony Tony saw children laughing as they sat on the Ferris Wheel.

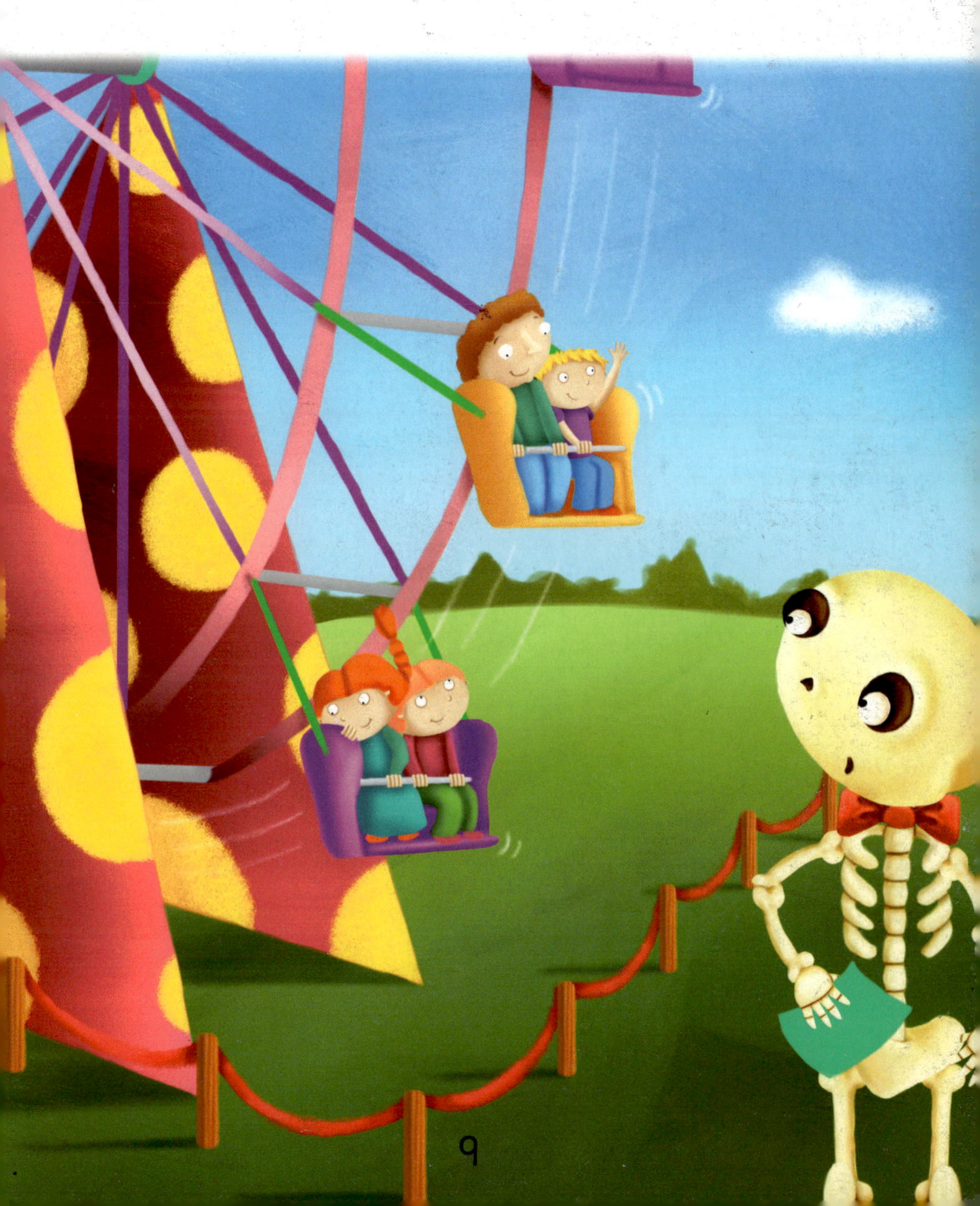

Just then, Bony Tony spotted the Twister. It zoomed round and round very fast.

“Wow!” he exclaimed. “I want a go on that!”

“OK,” said Skelly Nelly. “I’m going to buy some candyfloss.”

Bony Tony reached the
front of the Twister line.

"Fifty pence," said the Twister man.

Bony Tony had no money.

"No money, no ride," said the man.

Skelly Nelly reached the front of the candyfloss line.

"Fifty pence," said the candyfloss lady.

Skelly Nelly had no money.

"No money, no candyfloss," said the lady.

Skelly Nelly and Bony Tony were upset. They didn't know what to do.

Just then, a little boy came out of the ghost train tunnel.

"That wasn't a scary ghost train,"
he said.

"We want our money back,"
said the boy's dad to the ghost
train man.

Skelly Nelly and Bony Tony ran over to the ghost train man.

"We can make your ghost train scary," they said.

"Real skeletons!" exclaimed the ghost train man. "Perfect!"

Skelly Nelly and Bony Tony ran into the tunnel.

It was very dark inside.
All they could see were some plastic skeletons and a pair of paper ghosts.

“These aren’t scary!”
laughed Bony Tony.

st then, a car chugged
to the tunnel.

Skelly Nelly danced along beside it, rattling her bones.

"Aagh!" screamed the people. "A dancing skeleton!"

Another car chugged into the tunnel.

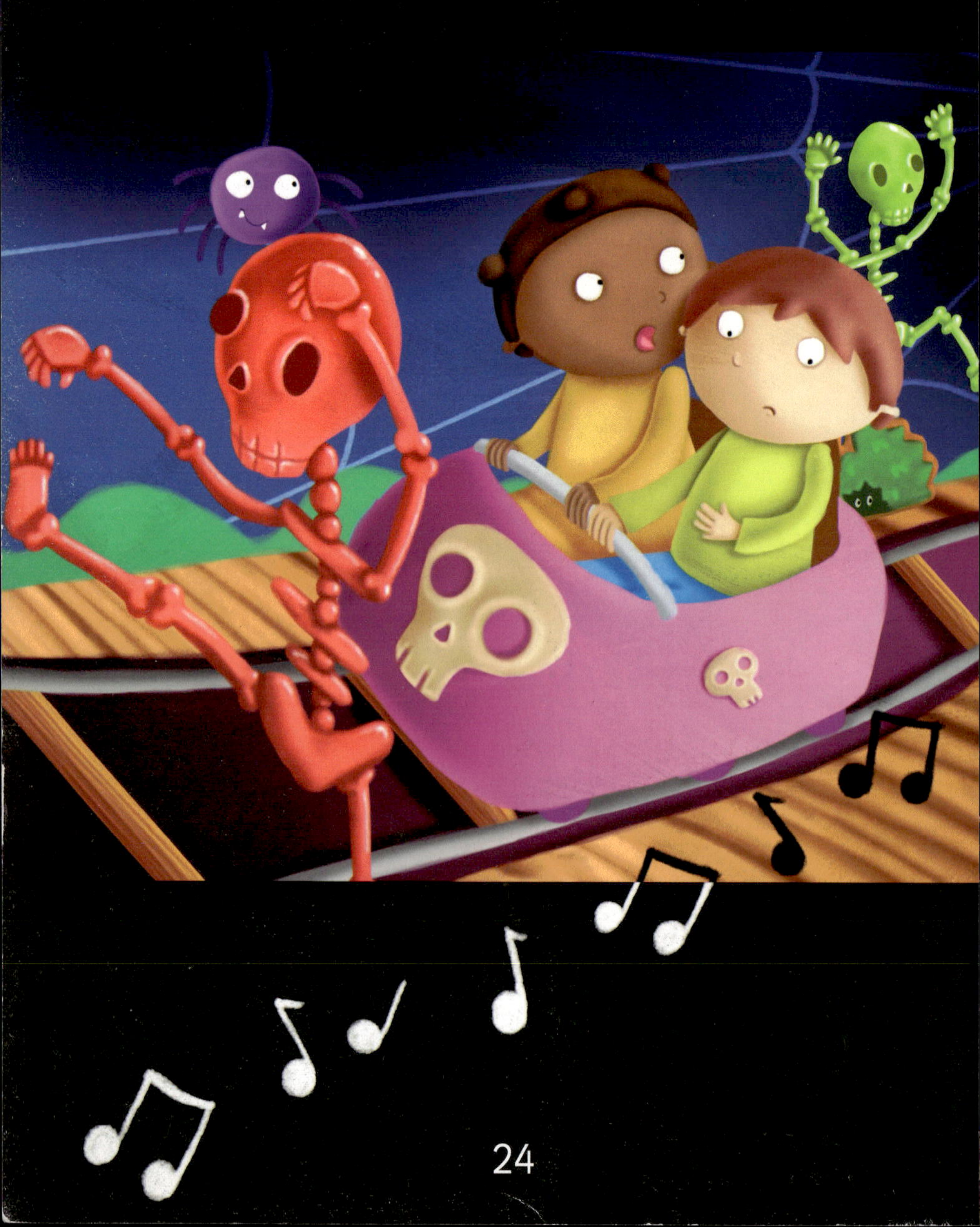

“Aagh!” the people cried.
“Who is making that noise?”

When the next car chugged into
the tunnel, Skelly Nelly and
Bony Tony pulled scary faces.

“Aagh!” cried the children.
“Scary skeletons!”

Bony Tony and Skelly Nelly stayed in the tunnel all day.

At last the ghost train man came in.

"I'm closing now," he said. "Thanks for helping."

He gave Skelly Nelly and Bony Tony some money.
"Please will you come back tomorrow?" he asked.

"Of course!" said Bony Tony.
"It's been fun!"

"The fun's not over yet!" said Skelly Nelly. She ran to the candyfloss stall.

Bony Tony ran to the Twister ride.
"We can't wait for tomorrow!"
they laughed.

START READING is a series of highly enjoyable books for beginner readers. **The books have been carefully graded to match the Book Bands widely used in schools.** This enables readers to be sure they choose books that match their own reading ability.

Look out for the Band colour on the book in our Start Reading logo.

The Bands are:

START READING books can be read independently or shared with an adult. They promote the enjoyment of reading through satisfying stories, plays and non-fiction narratives, which are supported by fun illustrations and photographs.

Liss Norton loves growing organic fruit and vegetables in her garden in the Sussex countryside, as well as spending time with her grandchildren, Maddie, Arabella, Dominic and Theo. When she's not writing, gardening or grandchildren-ing, she likes visiting castles. One day she hopes to find a secret passage...

Michael Garton lives with his girlfriend Leanna and a dalmatian puppy called Kiba. He works from his creepy flat on the Wirral in England (it's not quite a castle yet but he's saving up for one). He has been illustrating children's books since 2004 and thinks that everyone should have as many creepy experiences as possible.